HAPPY CAT and MERRY CAT

Mary Catherine Rolston

Illustrator: Keith Cains

FriesenPress

Suite 300 - 990 Fort St
Victoria, BC, V8V 3K2
Canada

www.friesenpress.com

ISBN
978-1-5255-2483-7 (Hardcover)
978-1-5255-2484-4 (Paperback)
978-1-5255-2485-1 (eBook)

1. JUVENILE FICTION, ANIMALS

Distributed to the trade by The Ingram Book Company

DEDICATION

To all mothers who always
seem to know what their kids are doing.

THERE WERE TWO FRIENDS,

and like **twins**, much was the same.

Both were nine, spry and Catherine was their names.

They liked to climb. They liked to rhyme.

nicknames

were picked that they used all the time.

Happy **Cat**
AND
Merry **Cat,**

LOVED TO PLAY

giggling

and wiggling every single day.

They liked to dance. They liked to prance.

They liked to sing.

They always took a

chance.

BEST OF ALL

they liked to drink tea and eat,
munching on finger
food and cakes so

sweet.

THEY DRANK

cold tea.

They drank hot tea.
They drank from

teacups

looking bourgeoisie.

THEY PLAYED DRESS-UP

with **outfits** every day, sometimes pretending they were in ballet.

They wore big hats. They ran like

cats.

THEY WORE *tails* AND EARS,

SCURRYING LIKE **rats.**

They'd parade down the
street their heads held high.

HAPPY Cat and

MERRY Cat

WERE NOT SHY,

STOPPING AND PEERING IN THE HOUSE OF TEA,

faces pressed to the glass,
trying to see,

trays filled with finger foods
and pretty sweets,

people slowly

sipping tea

in chic seats.

Drooling, dreaming of delicate

delights,

these kiddie cats licked their lips;

one sad sight.

As guests left and passed by, the girls smiled

and bowed.

Then they'd sing and dance,

amusing the crowd.

"Are you movie stars?" people asked in awe.

They were very impressed at what they saw.

The Catherines blushed, tossing back their

heads full of curls.

"Can you hold a secret? We're just wee girls.

If you have spare change, you can drop it there.

Tea, fruit, scones and strawberry jam we'll share.

Our high-tea dream will finally come

true."

THEIR LARGE TEAPOT OF CHANGE STEADILY GREW.

Days later, with coins spilling from the **top,**
the two jolly cats entered the **teashop.**
Dressed in their finest princess attire,
they announced it was high tea they desired.

The owner chuckled, saying, "Come this way."
Merry Cat gasped passing a huge bouquet.
Happy Cat grinned, seeing scones, squares and **cream,**
whispering, "Pinch me. Am I in a **dream?"**

Seated, Merry Cat passed the full **teapot.**
"We hope this is enough, it's all we've got."
The owner smiled. "This is more than enough.
Sandwiches, scones, squares, fruit, tea and cream **puffs**

will tickle your taste buds and fill your

tum."

Both sat straight, folding their hands and crossing their

thumbs.

Their wide eyes rolled trying
to soak up the pretty decor,
ladies with pinkies up holding
teapots as they poured.
A spectacular three-tiered
tray arrived with tea.
The girls' eyes popped

they

GIGGLED WITH GLEE.

Adjusting their napkins,
pinkies held high,
they began gorging on
delicacies.
They **certainly**
WEREN'T SHY!

Licking, smacking, while humming, "Mmmm, *yum!*"

they didn't notice standing behind them were their frowning **mums.**

"Catherine and Catherine, we've been looking everywhere!

You disappeared. We were worried. Don't you care?"

Both stopped and stared, like two squirrels caught munching with **zeal,**

chewing and swallowing before beginning their apology **spiel.**

"Sorry, Mom," blinked Happy Cat.

"Sorry, Mom," said Merry Cat,

adding, "We did yell out before we shut the door.

We didn't think you needed anything

more."

Their eyes downcast filled with tears.

They sighed, saying, "You know the food is delicious

here!"

The moms shook their heads and rolled their *eyes.*
"We are glad you are safe and sound. But you need to be *wise.*
Before you leave, you need to see us face to face.
We need to know what you are doing and the place.
By the way, where did you get the money to pay for lunch?
It looks like it has been crunched and munched."

Happy Cat smiled wide and proud and said, "We sang and *danced!"*
Just then the owner piped in, "Everyone leaving was entranced!
These wee busking ladies did earn this huge pot of *change.*

They presented it, requesting high tea in exchange."
The owner winked and continued, "It covered

the bill.

Serving these tea divas has been a thrill.
Please have a seat I will bring you

some tea."

"WHERE DID YOU GET THOSE FANCY HATS?"

"Why are you both so dressed up?"
asked each of the Cats.
The moms winked and chuckled,
"News in a small town travels quick."
"We have ways of keeping track
of you gals in our bag of tricks."

As the moms sat, the girls giggled with glee.
That afternoon, the girls' dream came

true.

THEY ALSO LEARNED A SAFETY LESSON TOO!

CPSIA information can be obtained
at www.ICGtesting.com
Printed in the USA
LVHW05s1534050518
576068LV00002B/2/P

9 781525 524844